RUSSIA HAS FALLEN

**...the war in the Middle East and Ukraine has
spread to Moscow!...**

by Semisi Pone

This book is dedicated to all men and women who have fallen in wars and conflicts throughout the world. May their sacrifices and lives be remembered forever...

CONTENTS.

Chapter 1. The Lovers

James and Angelique lay under the tent completely naked, next to each other. They were breathing heavily and holding hands, sweating in the mid-day heat. She turned her head to look out to the blue haze of the Mediterranean so the slight breeze can caress and cool her face. He kissed the back of her neck then spit out the bits of grass in his mouth.

"That was great darling. You have never been that passionate before, its as if you will never see me again!".

She sat up and looked down at him brushing her long black her away from her pretty face. She has tears in her eyes. She bowed down and kissed him passionately on the lips and got on top of him, making love to him again slowly grinding her whole body against his and moaning softly in his ear until she screamed her head off...her whole body going rigid...wretched with spasms.

He too cried out and squeezed her shaking body to his. She lay on top of him and tried to catch her breath again, then whispered into his right ear.

"I am leaving with our group tonight. We will be moving out of the Middle East. Our Commander has received new orders to assemble at the runway in the desert in Area 1. We will be dropped off in Russia. Just inside the border".

He sat up quickly as she fell off.

"What? Is he crazy? You cannot go into Russia without provoking them to retaliate!".

She shrugged her shoulders and stood up. He lay back again on the dry grass and admired her lean body. She is the most beautiful girl he has had the pleasure of meeting. He knew she is a spy.... and dangerous....but even spies also need love sometimes. And he provided love and affection for her.

He was a Scientist working in Kenya when he met her. She was with the French Legionnaires then joined the Red Cross. She was working in Kenya when they met. He was injured in the jungle one day when he fell off a rock cliff. She came with the First Aid group and uplifted him to the nearest hospital which was more like a jungle camp, where she looked after his injured leg. One night he woke up and she was sitting by his side in a chair, he thought she was an angel and he reached over to touch her. She took his hand and put it on top of her shirt, on her breast.

"What are you staring at, darling?", she smiled as she dressed putting on her pants with no underwear....as usual. Then army shirt and hat. He smiled to himself. She has been out in the field for so long....she has forgotten what Paris looks like. She has even lost her French accent and now has a Kenyan accent. Together with her good looks and martial arts skills...they picked her for the secret missions in the Middle East....and now Russia! He decided to

follow her. He has nothing else to live for.
She is his only family now and he knows
she may not come back from this one. There
has been rumors amongst the unit that the
Russians has been bankrolling the war in the
Ukraine and the Middle East to divert the
Americans and the British from the gas and
oil reserves in the Middle East that Russia
wanted to develop. The word is that....the
reserve is so big, it dwarfs the Saudi
Arabian oil supply. The problem is that, no
one knows exactly where it is. The terrorists
are just getting in the way of everyone and
keeping them out of the area.

"Darling, if you keep staring at me...I might
slap you to wake you up". She laughed in
her high tingling voice.

"Sorry, just thinking of the future". He said
it like a question as if to ask her what is
going to happen to them. He cannot live
without her now that they have been
together for 3 years.

"You should put on your clothes or I might

take mine off again". She smiled and walked out of the camouflaged tent. She raised the binoculars and scanned the Mediterranean Sea. Their job was to watch the ship movements along the coast of the Gaza strip.

They are to be air lifted that night from Gaza on the Israeli coast to Samsun on the Black Sea coast of Turkey.

"Honey, can I come with you? You know I cannot stay here, even if they send another girl to work with me".

He said it deliberately and watched her face closely. She was looking out to sea but she turned , sharply, to look at him.

"Don't you dare!".

Then she turned to look through the binoculars again. He got the message. She did not like what he said.

It is because he wants to protect her. Their

unit are all males and he does not like an all male unit working in secret with Angelique without his knowledge. Besides, no one knows anything about him. She tells them he is on a secret mission. He had been picked up by a boat arranged by her from the coast of Egypt and deposited on the coast of Israel at night. She met him and took him to her outpost. She had send off 2 other women soldiers who were working with her. He understood why when he arrived. She was hungry like a leopard at night.

He had been trained in Africa by some para-military outfit somewhere in the Congo jungle, arranged by her before they flew him to the coast. So he is becoming dependent on her.

"Alright. You can come with us".

She sat down beside him and put his hand inside her army shirt on her breast.

It was dark when they were finally satisfied

and had their fill of each other. It was a kind of reaction to danger. Almost like how endangered species react to negative selection pressure....by producing more offspring.

They took their backpacks and started walking towards Area 1 as darkness fell. It would be their last assignment in Israel. The Israelis will pickup the camouflaged tents and all the equipment, heavy artillery and grenades they cannot carry.

The cover story was that it was a UN training mission for two British secret service agents. The British have recently joined the war against ISIL and ISIS in Syria and Iraq. They are training their reconnaissance unit in Israel, learning desert warfare from the Israelis who are reputed to be the best in the Middle East.

After walking for half an hour they can hear the private jet coming in. They are to be flown to Turkey in a private commercial jet owned by an American business man. They have to cross Syria into Turkey so a military aircraft will attract suspicion. There is too much friction in the Middle East to risk flying a military aircraft from Israel through Syrian airspace. ISIL have control of a large territory there. The plane will just avoid it.

The plane roared briefly and came to a stop as they reached the top of the hill and came down towards the runway. It was one of the Israeli's best kept secret. They fly everywhere from that airstrip, because no one knows it existed. The aircraft used are all commercial ones and does not attract any attention, but inside the aircraft....they are all military personnel with military gear.

There was a group already assembled on the tarmac. They all look like SAS men in SAS uniform. A small hangar on the side serves as terminal with some people coming in and out of it.

"We need to get cleaned up and changed before we join them. I will meet you outside on the tarmac in 10 minutes". She said..... as

she hurries towards one side of the terminal.
They both know where the showers are.

The men on the tarmac were busy
discussing something and they all turned
and looked at them. She waved and pointed
at the showers...and they turned back to their
conversation. They all knew who she is.
And they all know who he is....but they all
pretend that he is a "trainee"....as she always
introduce him.

Chapter 2. The Meeting

The private jet took off without incident.
They flew off towards Lebanon and turned
into Syrian airspace. Everything has been
arranged by the Americans. It was an
American businessman visiting Turkey with
a brief stopover in Israel. The Syrians know
of their plane, in case somebody makes a
mistake with a surface to air missile.

They did not want to fly over the Gaza strip
or the West Bank.. Some terrorist might get
lucky with a machinegun or worse.

Angelique had arranged for them to sit in
the backseat so she can brief her "trainee"
on their mission. She fell asleep even before
they were halfway through Syria with her
head resting on James's shoulder. He could
smell her perfume, although they are not
allowed to wear any during missions. He
thought maybe because they will arrive in
the morning and will be sent straight to their
sleeping quarters. She knows he likes that
particular scent and she puts it on any

chance she gets when they are together.

He turned her head slightly to look at her face and could not help kissing her. She has that effect on him. She opened her eyes and looked at him. "Wanna have something to munch on? I have some sandwiches in my back. I made them in the terminal before we left. I don't know how long the flight will be. It might be several hours".

"Ok. I will fish them out when I am hungry. You can sleep". He smiled at her thoughtfulness. She is beginning to take care of him now.

Angelique smiled up at him. She has become soft after meeting him. She wonders what will happen if they get separated. She knows that war is coming to Russia and they will be in the middle of it. They will watch the shipping on the Black Sea for a while then move into Georgia. Their unit will be briefed in Georgia before they cross over into Russian territory. Their mission is so secret, they do not know what it is yet. She drifted off to sleep.

James could not sleep. He was looking out
the window to try and spot lights from any
of the cities in Syria or Turkey. It was all
black. He suspected they are flying over the
desert areas where no cities or even a house
can be found. The private jet was very
smooth. Not even a sound can be heard....or
his ears are blocked from the altitude like
flying in the large airliners. Then he drifted
off to sleep too.

Commander George Williams shook them
awake. They were already parked outside a
small terminal. They have no idea where it
is. They were told to get their gear and
assemble outside on the tarmac as an army
bus rolled up. An army Sergeant by the
name of Mike Hassan came around with a
pack of food for everyone as the bus stopped.

"The bus trip will take a few hours so it is
breakfast". He said as he hands them out.

"It must be early morning. I can feel the chills". James whispered to Angie as he calls her when they are intimate.

"Yeah. I can feel it too. Or maybe we are high up in altitude". She said as she surveys the group. There were 15 of them. They all wear army uniforms or slacks with army back packs. They look like a pack of commandos in the faint electric lighting. Their plane was parked some distance from the terminal so it must be a commercial terminal. There was no one around except the security guards patrolling around the perimeter.

"Ok everyone. We are to travel by bus to our destination. Please remember to take all your belongings from the plane as it will be leaving in a few minutes". Commander Williams said as he surveys the group. "Major Angelique Royal can you introduce your trainee please?". He said as he looks in her direction.

"Everyone, this is Major James Bonarparte

of the French Foreign Legion. You have all met him at some stage in the past". She looked up at him then smiled, her eyes twinkled. He knows she is very proud of him.

"Hi everyone". Major Bonarparte took off his beret and they all raised theirs is reply.

"Let's go, then". Commander Williams barked out the order as he got on the bus. He noted they do not have any French accent like most of the French secret service people he has worked with.

Sergeant Hassan came by and shook their hands as they queued up to the bus. "I will be the food manager in all situations and more....if you need any sustenance of any sort just let me know". He gave them a wink then boarded the bus.

James and Angie chose to sit at the back of the bus, as usual. They just want to enjoy each other's company for as long as possible.

Once they get into combat situations things might be different. It will be a matter of survival first. Cuddling and kissing will take the back seat.

The bus took off, only the headlight's powerful beams illuminating the road enveloped by an oppressive, cold darkness.

Angie put her head on James's left shoulder as they jolted around on the back seat. The road was full of potholes. Only small ones but it was still enough to make their trip uncomfortable. It was a country road heading down to the coast of the Black Sea somewhere near the Turkish town of Samsun.

They decided to have their breakfast. It was wrapped in aluminium. Hot baby potatoes and carrots with lamb and gravy. It was delicious.

"Sergeant Hassan must be an accomplished chef. James commented as Angie tries to finish hers. It was designed like an airplane meal but much bigger.

"Hmmm, it tastes really good".Angie whispered.

The bus came to a sudden stop in the middle of a pine forest.

"Everyone out". Commander Williams shouted from his seat at the front. "Head for the trees".

James and Angie reacted so fast, they were even surprised themselves. They threw their backpacks out the side window of the bus and followed them on to the grassy roadside. They picked up their backpacks in the same movement and bolted for the trees.
They jumped into the bushes under the large pines when the bus exploded. They were still on their stomach holding their backpacks when they can hear the debris whistling past them.

After about 5 minutes lying on the ground, they were confident enough to stand up.

Only the burning body of the bus and the flames crackling in the still darkness can be heard.

"Are you all right honey?". James whispered in Angie's left ear.

"What?"...she cannot hear him. The blast has temporarily blocked her ear.

He spoke louder. "Are you alright?".

"Yes, I guess so". She was shaking.

He pulled her towards him and hugged her for a long time. The darkness enveloping them as the flames grew smaller.

"I have heard that sound before", he whispered to her. "in the jungle in Congo".

"I know that is a Russian made coin-bomb. All our personnel knows them. A small coin-bomb the size of a box of matches can blow up a busload full of people. It can be hidden anywhere. I think Commander

Williams may have detected it when it was about to blow up. That is the only giveaway, it makes a peeping sound like air escaping from a balloon. That was close. I guess somebody does not want us to reach the coast".

"Yeah". Angie was shaking uncontrollably.

"Everyone, walk 100 paces into the trees with arms at the ready. Then report to me by calling out your names", Commander Williams voice broke the still darkness.

James and Angie got out their sub-machine guns handed out to them in the plane, from their backpack.   These Secret Service weapons usually have no markings on them. Some are new but already tested. They were more like pistols than machineguns. About the size of a small cordless drill with a "fat" barrel where up to 100 bullets can be loaded. It also has a laser which can also be used like a torch. They pointed the laser towards the interior of the forest and started counting their paces   watching everything ahead and behind them.

It seemed like an eternity to walk 100 paces into the forest. It was even colder and darker. It must have been an hour before they counted the last step then shouted out their first names. If anyone is listening it would be a giveaway. They did not plan on this happening. They did not have any ID numbers they can use. Their unit was brand new.

The group's names were being shouted out one by one. Only the driver was missing.

"It must be a suicide bomber". Angie whispered. "He was sitting at the front and he could have gotten out first".

"Logical". James whispered back.

"Alright everyone move towards me with arms at the ready". Commander Williams barked out the order then lighted a small beacon and stuck it on the ground.

Once they assembled Commander Williams confirmed that it was a suicide bomber and there is no one else around. They have to walk the rest of the way, arms at the ready.

Suicide bombers are usually the work of ISIL and ISIS and not the Russians. They all knew what that means. ISIL and ISIS knows of their mission!

They all picked up their backpacks and started down the road single file with sub-machine guns at the ready. Commander Williams produced a map and worked out that it will be another 100 kilometres walk to the coast. In their army boots it will be slightly uncomfortable but they are designed for heavy duty missions so they will last the distance on the gravelly road. It was forests on both sides of the road all the way. They have no choice. If there is an ambush ahead, they will just deal with it when they get there.

"If something happens up ahead stay close to me". James whispered to Angie as they got onto the road. Just follow me at 2 paces and be prepared to dive onto the roadside".

"Excuse me trainee. I am the Boss here. Remember?". Angie smiled up at him.
He felt a bit better and started down the road following the others.

An hour later, the sun came up. Sergeant Hassan must be a cooking genius. They walked for about half a day before they felt like drinking or eating.

"Alright everyone. Lunch time". Sergeant Hassan sang out and Commander Williams announced they head into the trees for lunch. Sergeant Hassan produced some packed sandwiches from his backpack. It does not take much to feed 15 hungry soldiers. He knows he can feed them with one loaf of bread with some nutritious fillings.

They were sitting among the trees in the shade munching on their sandwiches and watching the road. Then they heard it. The sound of a vehicle approaching fast from where they came.

Angie crawled to the tree edge and pulled out her binoculars. She motioned them to come closer and have a look. She gave them the "cut-throat" sign. They know its an enemy vehicle.

They hurriedly finished their sandwiches and crawled to the edge and looked down the road. It was a dark coloured double cap with a mounted machinegun on it, similar to what ISIS and ISIL are using in Syria. They have followed them into Turkey! They know they survived the blast and are coming after them to finish the job. There must others behind them. They also know the locals maybe looking the other way or pretending not to know anything.

"What's a coin bomb James?" Angie whispered as James lay down beside her.

"Oh, it is just a normal bomb with a powerful explosive the size and shape of a large coin. It is a new invention by some

Scientist in Russia". James whispered back as he looks around to see who is around them.

All the men were standing behind them watching the double cab with guns at the ready. They look like they are ready for a fight. They looked at Commander Williams, but he shook his head.

"Now is not the time to fight". He whispered.

Chapter 3. ISIL

The Syrian town of Al Qamishli near the Turkish border is about 800 kilometres from Samsun on the Turkish Black Sea coast. It can be 2 days drive at 80 km. Commander Williams has worked out they must be near the town of Kavak about 50 kilometres from Samsun. The problem now is how can they get around these ISIL fighters? He knows they must be from Al Qamishli as it has been known to be one of the ISIL bases to launch any "excursions" into Turkey. Their intelligence information indicates that it will be the headquarters of ISIL if Turkey becomes involved in the war. The reason is simple, because they control the entire area all the way to Iraq, which is about 100 kilometres away. Only half a day's drive from Al Qamishli in the rough terrain. Only 1-2 hours drive on a good road.

The Islamic State of Iraq and Syria (ISIS) is getting larger both in territory and manpower. They now control half of Iraq and Syria. An area the size of Uganda at

250,000 square kilometres with as many as 20 million inhabitants. Probably most of that population will gladly take up arms for ISIS.

"I suggest we lie low and assess the enemy strength before we move from here". Commander Williams whispered as the double cab passed with about five heavily armed men, one at the front with the driver and four at the back, with a mounted machine gun on it...which can also be used as an anti-aircraft gun.

"Corporal Quince, why don't you stay here and watch the road? We are going to retire further into the forest and do a pow-ow".

"Aye, aye, Sir". Corporal Quince whispered loudly and saluted while on his stomach watching the double cab through his binoculars.

Everyone crawled back into the forest and sat around Commander Williams.
"Alright, listen up. I know you have not been informed of our mission. The plan was

to inform you and show you our target in Moscow when we get to Georgia". Commander Williams paused for effect. There was an audible gasp from the group.

Somebody whispered..."Moscow?".

"Yes". Commander Williams whispered back. "I was given the plan just before we left in case something goes wrong and it has".

"Sir, does this mean we will not be going to Samsun?", Angie asked.

"Yes we will, but we will take a different route. We will have to go through the forest instead of the road. I have been given alternative routes for that very purpose. But we will leave Turkey as soon as we get to the Black Sea, now that the enemy has followed us. And you know there are a large number of them. Turkey is also a Moslem country and there will be a lot of ISIS sympathizers in the local population so we are in great danger already. We will go by boat across to Sokhumi on the Georgian coast and travel on land across to Russia to rendezvous with our contact at Maykop a small town in Russia. We will be airlifted from there to Moscow which is about 1,000 kilometres away. I will tell you the rest of the plan there". Commander Williams paused for effect. His bushy blonde moustache giving him the look of a Russian horseman with his fur hat on.

"Alright. It seems you all understand. We will cross the road and go through the forest to a trail which links up with others all the way to Samsun. Only about 60-70km as the crow flies".

Commander Williams stood up and put on his backpack.

"Alright Quince, follow us".

"Aye, aye, Sir". Corporal Quince jumped up and put on his backpack.

"Quince come close to me...I need you to

follow us and check these places out. Once we get to Sokhumi you are to drop back and use this map. Go straight to Kaluga, Tula then Samarra....you will be met over there and given further instructions in case you might have to rescue us..."

"Aye, aye, Sir".

They have crossed the road after the terrorists have passed and disappeared down the road. They dare not fire on them as it would give away their position and bring in more unpleasant characters. They know the forest is full of tracks large enough for vehicles, and there are more than one terrorist vehicle looking for them.

They are highly trained and well armed.

Walking through the trees was pleasant enough. The accumulated pine leaves provides a cushion on the ground. Except for the odd twig breaking they were as quiet as a painting. They found the track leading to Samsun and walked down single file. It was wide enough for a vehicle. They all know what to do if a terrorist vehicle appears. They were trained for it all their lives.

An American named Tim Craig dropped back and asked James if he has any communication gear. They know the French Foreign Legion soldiers sometimes carry satellite phones. They are the same size as mobiles but work on a satellite positioning system (SPS) instead of the local area network (LAN) system.

"What do you have in mind?". James asked. Normal security questions followed. Even in operations like this James has to suspect everyone, simply because he does not know who they are....and in the secret service, you can work with enemy agents for years without suspecting anything.

"I spoke to Commander Williams. We have to change mode of travel as the enemy may have compromised our plans. I will ask for a submarine to take us to Odesa in Ukraine instead of the fishing trawler planned for Sokhumi in Georgia. We have some friends in Ukraine, they will arrange for a submarine to pick us up somewhere near Samsun and take us ...then we can be airlifted from Odesa to Podol, a small town outside Moscow".

"Ok". James took out a small black box which looked like a case for an expensive pair of reading glasses. He blew on the surface for a few seconds and some letters appeared on it which he then pressed in a coded sequence. An aerial came out of the top and a build in microphone screen appeared on the surface.

"You can talk into it normally in English and they will connect you to where ever and whoever you want to talk to. It is coded and secure. No one can intercept your message". James handed his satellite phone to Tim. "Just press the green spot near the mike screen when you want to talk and when you finished talking. They will ask you questions if they need to, otherwise, it is all your instructions. This spot on the other side of the mike screen will light up if they have received and successfully conveyed your message".

"Thanks James. I owe you one". Tim smiled brightly as if he just landed on the moon.

"Don't worry about it. We're in this together".

"I will drop back a few paces to arrange it. Just make sure you keep an eye on me, while I talk". Tim nodded and started talking into the mike as he paced backwards.

"Ok". James took out another piece of equipment which is a camera attached to the back of his cap and sunglasses. He can watch Tim while he talks on the phone. There might be an ambush.

"You didn't tell me you have a satellite phone", Angie said accusingly.

"Well, everything is a secret until you need

to know". James smiled and gave her a wink.

"I'll keep that in mind". She said frostily and moved ahead of him.

The team were making good progress down to Samsun when they heard another vehicle. They all turned and bolted quietly into the trees.

This time it was a Toyota pickup similar to a 2 tonne hiace. A very popular work vehicle in Asia. There were more than 10 armed fighters sitting on the back looking into the forest with sub-machine guns similar to AK 47s but the latest Russian made ones.

They hid behind the trees.

The mini-truck passed and Commander Williams called them together.

"I saw one guy with a radio. So we have to maintain complete silence there may listening devices hidden on the roadsides".

Tim handed the satellite phone back to James. "Everything is arranged". He gave him the thumbs up as they moved back on to the road.

Commander Williams was busy looking at his map trying to ascertain where they were and how far they are from Samsun. They must have walked for an hour or so.

He waved everyone to the side of the road. "I think we should lie low here in the forest and move down to Samsun tonight. There may be more terrorist vehicles joining the search. It is too risky to go on".

Everyone agrees, and they all move further into the forest and prepare camp.

"Quince, our plan is cancelled...you come with us". Commander Williams whispered to Quince as he sidled up to him.

"Aye, aye Sir".

Chapter 4. The PLO

When Yasser Arafat was the leader of the Palestinian Liberation Organisation (PLO) for most of its existence since 1964, their dream was to force or negotiate with Israel, and the rest of the world, a homeland for the Palestinians. They had a legitimate claim as most of the founders were former residents of Palestine, now Israel. Although the population of Israel includes Jews, Druze, Sunni Moslems and Christians; the PLO believes that they should have a separate state.

There were many terrorist acts committed in the name of the PLO including the famous Black September massacre of the Israeli Olympic team in Munich, West Germany in 1972. Many of the world's countries condemned the violent actions of the PLO which culminated in the death of Yasser Arafat on 11 November 2004 at his home known as the Arafat Compound in Ramallah, Westbank; amidst accusations of plutonium poisoning. It has been under restriction by the Israeli army for 2 years.

Although Yasser Arafat actively promoted diplomacy as the way forward, it was essential for the PLO to make their point. The world have to take their claims seriously and they were willing to sacrifice many lives to achieve their goals. Suicide bombings in Israel and other atrocities finally led to their recognition by the UN as a State. Although there are still factions within the State of Palestine who are still not satisfied and still claim that the State of Israel should be destroyed because the land belongs to them.

The majority of the UN countries, however, believes that peace will come sooner rather than later.

The United Nations recognised Palestine as a State in the Gaza strip and West Bank. The State of Palestine has full representation in the United Nations General Assembly. They are being encouraged to move forward through education and developing their

country rather than sacrificing their children
in the name of winning against Israel which
will never happen. The Allies will not
accept it whatever form it may take whether
it be war or diplomacy.

That was the main reason why James and
Angie became involved. They were
supporters of a better deal for everyone in
the region both in Israel and the Gaza strip.
They chose to fight the terrorist elements
who, rather than fighting for a cause, are just
disrupting the peace process. Everyone
suspects a world power with unlimited
resources is backing the terrorists, who seem
to have large amounts of cash and weapons
all the time. They now believe it to be the
Russians or a group within Russia with
commercial interests in the Middle East, and
who resent the influence that the United
States, the British and their allies   have in
the region.

Tim was reading through some notes that
James made. "I did not know you are a
soldier of fortune". Tim was looking at

James expecting some answers about his involvement.

"You know the drill Tim. Everything is a secret until you need to know". He gave Tim a smile and looked back at his tiny laptop. It is only the size of a diary, about as thick and powered by human body warmth or solar energy. James simply put the panel in his shirt against his body and his body temperature heats up the panel and is converted into electrical energy and stored in the computer battery.

"You seem to have all the modern gadgets James. Where did you buy the laptop?". It was another searching question. James feel the American is jealous or simply trying to provoke him.

"No hard feelings Tim, but I think you need to shut up. There might be listening devices around the trails". James gave Tim a cold stare and Tim looked away.

They have been sitting around the camp for

almost 5 hours so maybe the inactivity is getting to Tim.

It was getting dark and they started packing. Sergeant Hassan came around with more sandwiches. Everyone got a sandwich and a can of pure fruit juice. They need their energy as the next meal will be in the submarine, whenever they get to it. If they fail to get on board they will be in trouble as there is no more food and drink left. They may have to raid a local supplier or store for food.

"Alright, everyone. Let's move out. Maintain silence until we get to the coast". Commander Williams moved out of the forest on to the road, which they can barely see in the dark. Everyone followed with their sub-machine guns ready to fire at any time.

James knows why they were given those new sub-machine guns. The bullets are made of a new explosive material which gives it more damaging power than normal bullets. It is a hush hush kind of weapon. It will be taken off them once the mission is over. They have been asked to hand them in to a certain General once they are back in London. After this mission, James and Angie will be free to retire from "the organisation". It is so secret, no one even knows it existed; including its employees. All employees of the organisation have a term of 20 years maximum or age 55 whichever arrives first. All employees must be fit and able to carry out missions all over the world. They usually deal with front "partners" of the organisation. James does not mind, but he wishes he knew more about it. He enjoys working for them and hope to work in management, if there is such a thing as the organization's headquarters. He is not paid in cash, all his needs are supplied. He will be given his "reward" when he decides to leave. It could be a retirement property anywhere in the world or a business to draw money from.

The single shot rang out like those in the movies. Not like the bark of a modern sub-machine gun but more like those rifles in cowboy movies. Tim fell silently like as if his heart and nervous system collapsed suddenly. His helmet hit the loose stones on the trail with a twang and rolled to the other side of the road. Everyone dropped and rolled to the side of the road sub-machinegun pointing at the other side. They cannot see a thing in the enveloping darkness.

James knew why. Tim was the only one wearing sand shoes. He had taken off his boots and put on his running shoes and its got fluorescent marks on them! He said the boots are too uncomfortable to walk with. The fluorescent   marks cannot be seen at 1-5 metres but it looks very shiny from 20-500 metres. Some terrorist saw it and shot him in the chest. He was not moving. The bullet must have pierced and burst his heart into a thousand pieces.

Lucky the shooter did not have a grenade launcher or machinegun. He could have gotten more of them!

"Does anyone know where that shot came from?", Commander Williams whispered to them loudly.

"No, Sir", Quince whispered back.

The silence was deafening. The sniper must be searching for the next victim with his sniper's rifle.

"Ok, lets crawl back into the forest. They will be waiting for us ahead", Commander Williams whispered back.

They crawled back into the trees. The grassy roadside feeling more comfortable than their sticky situation. Bruce, the other American on the team, is crawling back with a rope he has tied to Tim's foot. He wants them to pull his body up so they can bury him before they continue.

"Remove his shoes and leave them on the road", James whispered to him. "It's got fluorescent markings on them".

"Ok". Bruce whispered and he crawled back to the trail and removed Tim's shoes, being careful not to attract any attention by sudden movements of the shoes. He also tied his backpack to the rope then crawled back.

Five of them started pulling Tim's body up to the treeline while another 2 started digging a grave for him.

"After Tim's burial we have to move out of here quickly. They may be moving in as we speak". Commander Williams whispered loudly. James can detect sadness in his tone maybe he is crying. It was Commander George Williams who picked Tim for the mission. In fact he picked everyone except James who was picked by Angie as an addition.

The organisation gave Commander George Williams clearance for James at the highest level. In fact, Commander Williams was surprised that both the Pentagon and British intelligence had supported his selection.

Commander George Williams was a Colonel in the British Secret Service and a General in the British Army, whichever requires his services. Only 54 years old, he is fit and the most experienced of the 15 member team, except maybe one other.

That was why he prefers not to discuss too many things with the team members....only the barest and most essential details.

They dug a shallow grave for Tim and put his body and backpack in it, removing all identification items. They made a note of the global positioning point (GPP) so they can recover his body after, if required by his family. They found some stones and piled them on top to prevent wolves and other animals from digging up his body. They also put a crudely made cross stuck at one end, on it to warn every passer-by it is a human grave. Bruce Copper, Tim's American mate, said some prayers for Tim reciting the Lord's prayer then they moved out, putting on their night goggles to allow them to see in the dark forest.

James asked Bruce whether Tim gave him the details of their submarine meeting point, but Bruce said no he did not.

James asked Commander Williams and he said yes, he has the co-ordinates in his pocket. They are to move through the forest to about 10 kilometres from Samsun along the coast to Bafra. They are to make a satellite call to a certain number once they are on the coast. The submarine will send a small inflatable boat to pick them up within one hour of their call. After one hour the submarine will leave the area. If they do not make contact for some reason. They are to call another number and meet a certain American in Istanbul. The mission may be cancelled and replaced with another team. They will hand in all their gear and be dismissed due to security reasons. If asked about the mission from anyone, they are to deny everything.

James felt happy for some reason. He looked at Angie who was walking beside him with her sub-machinegun thrust forward. He hopes they will be dismissed. He already has some retirement plans for them. He thought about it as they moved through the silent giant trunks, looking like the terracotta army of the Chinese Emperor.

James thought of the PLO as they kept moving   throughout the night, Yasser Arafat was never involved in any of the actual terrorist acts himself. Although he was blamed for many of them. He was the diplomatic face of the organisation. They were highly organised and even encouraged by the West. There is something about them and the State of Palestine that keeps cropping up in his mind. He remembers that all the Arab leaders have pointed to Palestine as the problem. The "Palestinian question" they call it. Israel has gone out of its way to help them and help the State of Palestine get established but there is still terrorists in Palestine or the Gaza strip who are still firing rockets into Israel. Every time Israel retaliates, with devastating results for many houses in the Gaza strip or West bank, blown up by bombs from Israeli gunships and helicopters. Still the Palestinians kidnap or harm Israelis at every opportunity. There is a definite pattern to it. Somebody does not want peace between Israel and the Palestinians.

It was close to morning, the team can feel the fatigue coming on. They are also feeling hunger pangs. They started chewing on their emergency food supply which are mostly high energy dried food and drinking from their build in water supply in the backpacks.

Commander Williams called a halt. "Everybody, listen up". He whispers loudly. "We are about half a kilometer from the coast. I will get James to call the number Tim gave me for our rendezvous with the submarine. I estimate we will reach the coast in just under an hour, hopefully to meet the welcoming party. If not we are to travel to Istanbul, hand in our equipment at the British Embassy and disperse. You will be asked for your contact details in case they want to recall you in the future. Here's the number James".

James took the number, blew on his black box til the letters appear then key in the code. Once the aerial and mike appear...he started talking to them..."This is Jones at Madame Elizabeth's school....we are one hour away from the target, please send the welcoming party to meet us". He pressed the spot by the mike as the other side of it lights up. They got the message. Then it blinked 4 times. A special message for James.

He understood what they mean.

"They got the message", James said and he looked longingly at Angie who looked defiantly back at him from behind her night goggles. He thought, he will never understand her and her moods.

"Ok. Let's move", Commander Williams whispered.

They all formed a single file and moved forward together.

James felt that it is safe. The terrorists are well trained. They have probably assessed the situation and consider it none of their business to pursue them any further. Submarines and navy boats do have some very accurate guns that can blow up their double cabs and mini-trucks with one shot. They are not going anywhere near the coast and expose themselves to any fire from the submarine or boat. They will head back to Syria. They are very shrewd they know the commandos are meeting a boat or submarine, otherwise why are they hurrying towards the coast? Their mission must be very important or they would have picked a fight with them.

The terrorists have beaten them to the coast.

Commander Williams emerged from the tree line and saw a lone figure standing by the water about 50 metres away. He looks like a man dressed in Arab clothes. He has a gun, probably an AK 47, but he is looking out to sea. It was beginning to get lighter but he cannot make out who he is. Then he saw two others came out of the beach. He held up his hand and crouched.

"Looks like the terrorists got here before us. We have to fight it out or leave for Istanbul". He whispered loudly as he began to move forward. The others spread out and moved down closer to the water. There were more terrorists coming out of the beach. They came in by boat!

Commander Williams dropped on his stomach at about 30 metres and started firing. All the others did the same. They were shocked. Their sub-machine guns made very little noise! It was more like the spitting of a rifle with silencer than a sub-machine gun! Several of the terrorists on the beach fell as their bodies were smashed in half by the hail of sub-machine gun bullets. James can actually see bits of their bodies and arms flying off as they got hit! They look like dark objects against the light background of the sea surface as the sky lights up with dawn.

Then the terrorists started firing back. James counted about 20. The fire spitting out of the gun barrels can be seen clearly. He can hear the whistling of the bullets just above his head. The terrorists are lying flat on the ground just above the beach.

James can also see the periscope of the submarine moving across the horizon. The others have seen it too. James took out his satellite radio and send the submarine a message. There are about 20 terrorists holding them up on the beach. They have killed more than 10 or so. Can they blow them up with their cannon? He gave them the directions and co-ordinates and waited.

The submarine surfaced slowly as if in a movie. Then 2 flashes on its deck can be seen. James counted and did not get to 5 when the whole beach seem to erupt into the heavens with terrorists bodies flying high into the light morning sky. He is always amazed how technology have made these guns so deadly and accurate.

James send another message. "Bulls eye".

They saw an inflatable being lowered and they started moving down to the beach as the dust clears and blown off by the slight breeze. Their ears still ringing from the blast, even though they always use ear plugs.

"About time you turned up". Colonel John Bridge said to James as they walked down the beach avoiding the terrorist bodies and parts lying on the sand and rocks. He came off the inflatable and was holding a rope tied to it, with another soldier holding a sub-machine gun on the boat and keeping the engine going.

"Nice to meet you again John". James shook his hand. The last time he saw him was when he waved from their departing jeep as they left their camp in the Jungle in the Republic of Congo.

"Hi George. I thought you had retired". John was shaking hands with Commander Williams as everyone got on board and they started back to the submarine, just as daylight was breaking.

"I thought the same of you too". James heard George saying to John.

"Don't worry about the mess, our boys are on their way to clean it up. We don't want anything in the news, if you know what I mean". John Bridge was talking as he steered the inflatable back to the submarine. It was large enough for them with some spare space.

Everyone were shown their quarters and the submarine dived and disappeared into the dark waters.

Chapter 5. The IRA

James was reading a Hello magazine in his room. He has had a shower then helped himself to the food tray on the table. It was still hot. Potato mash, sausages, bacon, boiled vegetables and fruit juice and coffee.

There was a story in the magazine about Prince Charles hosting a dinner for the Retired Servicemen's Association (RSA) in London. The funds will be donated to the latest casualties from Iraq and Syria. Although most allied soldiers have left there were a small number of trainers and advisors left.

Then a small article caught his attention. President Vladimir Putin of Russia had to leave a G20 meeting in Brisbane, Australia, after an argument or disagreement with the other leaders over the war in the Ukraine and the Malaysian Airline MH17, which was rumored to have been shot down by the Russians or their supporters.

Another Malaysian Airline plane had disappeared only a few months before flying from Malaysia to China.

James knew what is going on. The Russians were under pressure at the G20 to withdraw their support for the terrorists in the Middle East and separatists in the Ukraine. The Secret Service has known about it for a long time, but it is the Politicians who make decisions on such sensitive issues. The Secret Service will not do anything other than advice the Governments of what is going on behind closed doors in the Kremlin. It is the Politicians who decide to do something about it or sweep it under the carpet.

He remembers, exactly the same thing happening with the Irish Republican Army (IRA). Even though they killed Lord Mountbatten and the Politicians knew about it, nothing was done. In fact, the Politicians could not do anything!

It was exactly a parallel of the Black

September attack on the Israeli Olympic team at Munich. None of the Politicians can do anything other than condemn their actions.

There were other "actions" that went on behind the scenes. A kind of cold war in both cases. The British decided to use the Secret Service to hunt down the IRA members and eliminate them. The Israeli Government also formed a special unit to hunt down the members of Black September and destroy them. And in both cases both organisations were decimated so much that both accepted Political solutions.

Sinn Fein, the Political Arm of the IRA, signed a kind of Peace Agreement with the British and the PLO accepted a kind of deal with the Israelis before they totally disappeared off the map or changed their name and structure to camouflage it.

In both cases the Political solution was the answer.

James can still remember talking to a Palestinian girl in Cairo, she was one of the most beautiful women he had met. She was a highly trained terror operator and he had to be careful. They had an affair for about a year before she was killed in a bomb attack on tourists in Cairo. He could not help feeling devastated when she died. He had promised her he would help the Palestinian cause in whatever way he can, and he is.

Palestine is now a recognised State, all they have to do now is find some peace with Israel and improve their political relationships with the superpowers and get some help to rebuild their lives. Unfortunately, there are still some terror groups who do not want peace. Some businesses in Israel do benefit from the conflict through high demand for war technology and arms.

James suspects it has something to do with this Moscow mission, whatever it is. Only Colonel George Williams knows what it is. And he was one of the Secret Agents who destroyed the IRA or brought them down to their knees....so James has a lot of respect for "the old man" as he is called, affectionately, by the members of their group.

James did meet some IRA operatives in Paris. They were after some high explosives which were not commercially available. The French had developed them for use in the civil war in Algeria in Africa. It is so powerful that an explosive the size of a marble can blow up a truckload of soldiers.

The word on the street was they are going to put them in microphones attached to the benches of Parliamentarians in the British Parliament. They had failed once and now they will not fail again. Even just one of those marbles can kill all the members of Parliament. James can imagine having 20 or more explode at the same time in the House of Commons or Lords. There will be nothing left! Only the rubble!

James's mission was to swap the marbles

after the sale in the Paris black market. The IRA paid $ 4 million British pounds or about $US 10 million for just 20 of the explosives! They were so small they were all canned with some sardines! The Black Market operators claim that the sniffer dogs will not be able to detect them in a can of sardines.

James did like the young men who collected the package! Although he had already swapped them. The IRA did come after the Paris Black Market operators and totally wiped them out. They never knew who had stolen their marbles.

James looked at his watch. They have been in the submarine for about 12 hours. It must be night time again. It's about 1,000 kilometres across the Black Sea from Samsun to Odesa so there may be a few more hours....maybe another 24 hours before they get there.

James looked at the list and rooms and decided to give Angie a visit. She has been angry with him so he hopes that maybe she miss him already. He came out of his room and walked down the corridor. It looks just like the corridors in the cruise liners. Only the rooms are a bit smaller with just the necessities. He knocked on the door of Angie's room. She opened the door and jumped outside. She kissed him and hugged him at the same time.

"Let's go inside". He whispered. "You don't want anyone to see us, right?". She giggled.

"Ok". She pulled him inside her cubicle and locked the door.

They made love all the way to Odesa.

"I cannot believe your appetite for love Angelique Royal!". He teased. "You want to have sex 23 times a day! I can't keep up! There is only a one hour break!". She laughed out loud. Her normal tingling laugh. He always enjoy listening to her laughing at his jokes....teasing her.

An announcement came they have to get ready to disembark. James kissed Angie and told her. "Whatever happens, always remember that I love you with all my heart. If we are still alive after this mission, please marry me?".

She smiled then laughed. Tears running down her whitish-brown cheeks. "Yes my darling, I will marry you. Even if we die, I will meet you in heaven....and marry you James Bonaparte, you cannot escape from me!". She burst into tears for a few minutes then dried her eyes and pulled herself together.

"You better go and get ready". She said.

"Ok". James kissed her and got out of the room.

Chapter 6. The Muslim Brotherhood

When James met Ada, she was only 17 years old. He was working in Cairo with the "organisation" and she has just been recruited by the Moslem Brotherhood. She is a Palestinian, born in the Gaza strip but educated in Egypt. Her family had high hopes for her. She was very bright and they had hoped she would get a good job and move the family to Cairo. They were sick of the conflict in the Gaza strip. There were deaths and destruction everyday. They want some peace for their kids and grandkids growing up in a peaceful country.

Then violence erupted in Egypt too. She was a foreigner studying in Cairo and although she is an Arab, they picked on her and persuaded her to become one of them. She believed in their cause, which was "freedom for all Moslems". She did not realise the huge sacrifice she has to make. James was in Cairo on a different mission and he was told about her. She is a bright kid with a bright future but persuaded to do evil by a misdirected and misinformed organisation.

He met her at the University and continued to meet her everywhere she went. She finally agreed to go out to dinner with him and do all the things teenagers in the West do....including falling in love and surrendering her virginity to the man she loves. She suspected who he is and what he does. She has been trained to recognise foreign spies working in Egypt and the Middle East. She was asked about him frequently by the Moslem Brotherhood, but she kept saying he is just a harmless friend. She knew one day she would be asked to kill him. She was hoping he would take her with him to Britain or United States before that.....then she can bring her family. They found out what she plans and ended it with a bomb destined to destroy the Tourism Industry....the biggest money earner for Egypt.

James had put on some clothes and packed his bag. He is just waiting for the call to disembark. He suspects that this mission is some kind of "proof gathering" mission from the Kremlin. The West wants some proof that Russia is backing the terrorists and separatists so they have justification for some action.

A note was send through the message tube. They will wait until dark to disembark or get airlifted from the submarine helipad whichever comes first. James is getting used to these either or arrangements. It is Commander George Williams kind of approach. There are always 2 or 3 plans at any time, and they are not really sure which one will be implemented until it happens. A very effective way of keeping any spies guessing otherwise there might be a surface to air missile waiting for them if there is only one plan and the enemy finds out.

The fate of MH 17 is still lingering in everyone's mind. This is a different kind of game. The Russians are much more advanced technologically than the rebels and terrorists.

James thought he will visit Angie because they have a few hours to kill.

She was eager as usual, loving, demanding, giving, with her eyes so full of darkness. He knows why....she is really scared of losing him. The only love she has known. A woman of great beauty, intelligence and bravery. She has faced so much hardship that she is as tough as any of the men. But her heart has become soft because of him and she fears losing him in action or to another woman. He knows she will kill to keep her man. After all, she will only live once. There won't be a second chance.

Ada was like that too. A beautiful woman who will kill anything and everything standing between her and the man she loves. He suspects that is why she died in the bomb. Her Moslem Brotherhood co-conspirators were scared of her. They know she loves him more than the cause and has to be eliminated. It was the beginning of the end for the Brotherhood. When they started turning on each other, the whole organisation collapsed with suspicion, assassinations and jealousy.

James has seen it before in other terrorist organisations. When the cause and their common goals are overlooked for other reasons. The members start to lose faith and either start leaving or shoot each other.

"What are you thinking of, darling?". Angie got up on her elbow and kissed him. "Just the mission and the past". He looks at her then smiles. Touching her cheek and lips. Its good to make love to a beautiful woman before you go to war, if you die she will be the last thing you remember. James smiles again, at the thought, and kissed her. Then they made love again on the small submarine bunk. Making sure they explore each others body throughly so there is no unknowns between them.

It was late afternoon when the next note came through the tube. "Get ready".

James kissed Angie a few times and got dressed then sneaked back to his room. He made a list and started checking everything to make sure he has everything he needs. Ada was always very meticulous with her preparations. He had learned that from her. That is why she was feared by the other members of the Moslem Brotherhood. She does not miss much and will shoot first and ask questions later when threatened. He remembers their last mission. It was the assassination of a certain famous terrorist in Paris. The terrorists were in Paris to buy some "marbles" from the French. They plan to send some to Washington inside an Egyptian diplomat. The plan was flawless.

The diplomat was to have corrective surgery to remove fat from his abdominal area in Thailand. The terrorist plan to fill his abdominal cavity with explosive marbles and detonate them in the Oval Office in the White House. They need special kinds of marbles that will not dissolve inside the abdominal cavity and cause any discomfort. He will accompany a group of "Peace

Lovers" to meet President Barrack Obama in the Oval Office with a celebration after on the White House lawn, 2 weeks later. Ada knew it is possible. Their plan could work.

Ada did not like the plan. She told James they have to kill them because it is not part of their cause. If they blow up the President of the United States, it will be the end of their cause and their families. A lot of other people will be killed too.....just like the British and Israelis dealing to the IRA and Black September, when Lord Mountbatten and the Israel Olympic team were killed. James agreed.
The only way to win the war is through diplomacy. You can win a few battles by blowing up and shooting the wrong people. It will just accumulate your enemies until they overrun your cause.

James has made sure that Ada understands that. Never shoot or kill anyone who is on your side! Only kill when you are threatened or have to. Indiscriminate killing of human beings however unimportant they are is not a good look if you want sympathy from the international community and support for your cause. And she did.

She was like Angie in a way. Beautiful, brave, tough as iron but with a soft spot for him. And he enjoys her attention and love for him. Even when under fire, he still thinks about their most intimate moments. One time in the desert, they were hunted by a group of Tuareg. The Tuareg were informed that 2 terrorists are in the area and must be eliminated at all cost.

James and Ada were hiding behind a rock up in the mountains of Ethiopia with more than a 100 Tuareg shooting at them. James thought that would be the end for them. It was one of many incidences when the satellite radio saved him and his co-fighters.

He kissed Ada and looked into her dark eyes. He held her warm soft body against his as he blew on the radio and punched the code in, as bullets were whistling past them. She knew what it was and she smiled up at him.

Half an hour later the shooting stopped and they could hear the sound of a helicopter.

It was the first time the Americans had saved him. Normally, it was Colonel John Bridge and his friends who were called in emergencies. There was an American company drilling for oil nearby and they were asked to pick them up from the mountains. They were two American geologists surveying the area. It was that easy.

That was the last time James went on a "pick up" mission. They went on two camels to pick up an operative who was lost in the desert, then got chased by more than a 100 Tuaregs with guns blazing when the camels were at full speed!. James knows they were set up.

The next message came. "Assemble on the helipad". Kames picked up his large bum bag and attached it. That was all he was required to carry. He just needs some warm clothes, sub-machine gun, satellite phone, some emergency medicine and dried food. His emergency water was build in to his jacket lining. He has 500 mls of purified water in case he needs it. They were to be airlifted from Odesa to Podol and meet the others there for a briefing before they get dropped off in Moscow.

The lights of Odesa looks really inviting from the top of the submarine. There was a slight breeze and it felt icy cold. James remembers it is approaching winter in the North Hemisphere. October is already cold enough for warm clothes and thick jackets at night.

Commander Williams motioned everyone to board the waiting helicopter. He does not like to talk and give any listeners more information. The helicopter took off into the dark cold night. It turned and headed towards Podol, more than 1,000 kilometers away. They might stopover a few times to refill on the way. Podol is perfect as it is a straight drive or flight into Moscow, about 100 kilometres or less. James suspects there will be others on this mission, the biggest he has been on.

The lights of Odesa seem to blink up at him. Vehicles look like ants hurrying around on the grid. Angie put her arm around James for comfort. She has become more like a lover than a spy as the mission progresses. James is getting a bit worried about her.

Their mission to Paris was the most dangerous he had been on. He and Ada had to eliminate more than 10 terrorists who are highly trained, armed and dangerous. Ada was perfect. She knows them and how they operate.

When the deal was made and the terrorist had their marbles, Ada made her appearance. Abdul, their leader, was shocked to see her in the hotel foyer. They were preparing to leave that night for Cairo. She told him they have come as extra security. Abdul resented it, a woman coming to protect him. He fumed, but did not show it. James was listening from outside.

Abdul invited Ada to his room to "view the merchandise". There were five other men there, in expensive suits, she has never met before. They showed her the briefcase with the marbles. They look like large shiny ball bearings. She nodded drew her automatic and shot Abdul on the forehead. He collapsed quietly on to the carpet.

The sudden loud bang shocked the others who have been standing about 5 metres away in the large suite. They dived for cover behind the large bed. She closed the briefcase, walked outside the room and threw a grenade into it and locked the door. The muffled sound of the explosion did not even attract any attention. The bullet proof doors and windows made sure of that. James and Ada put the marbles in a safe deposit box in a large bank in Paris, for future use, and flew to London for some sightseeing and catching up with old friends. The Secret Service cleaned up the room so no one even suspected anything.

"You were perfect in there". James complimented her. She smiled at him and kissed him on the lips as the Air Hostess passed them their earphones. "He would have shot me if I hadn't beaten him to it". She said and looked at him seriously and kissed him again. She put on her headphones and settled down to listen to Michael Jackson's "Gone too soon", closing her eyes and pulling the blanket up to her shoulders. She thought it is appropriate for the moment. A kind of melancholy but essential regret. The last thing they want is 10,000 US Secret Agents chasing them around the world. James looked out the window of the Airbus 380 and smiled. They got away with it without even sweating. The plane was still climbing into the clouds when they drifted off to sleep.

The helicopter was slowly losing altitude. The first refill will be in Kiev. Then they will cross the border into the Russian Federation and probably refill again before descending into Podol for the final briefing. The Russians have been informed they are a

group of Ukrainians on a business trip to
Moscow. All the papers were in order in
case they get stopped and asked within
Russia. Several of the team can speak
Russian fluently so they should not have any
problems.

James looked out the helicopter window at
some of the dark areas under them. He
always half expect the blazing trail of a
surface to air missile speeding up to meet
them. He suppose the Russians will not
shoot down civilians for no apparent reason.
Its true they may have shot down the
Malaysian Airline MH 17 plane but...maybe
they were secretly supporting the terrorist or
supplying funds to them. That is how it
usually works. "Pay back" as his friends
calls it in High School. Two MH flights 370
and 17 met some mysterious end within a
few months of each other....is very
suspicious. It stinks of a "Pay back" kind of
arrangement.

Finally, James drifted off to sleep and
dreamed of Ada making love to him while

Angie holds on to his side and even kissing him at the same time. He smiled in his sleep. Its nice to have 2 beautiful women love him. It lessens the feeling of danger and death. It increases his boldness in dangerous missions.

Chapter 7. The Pentagon

President Barrack Obama was sitting at the head of the table, looking around at the Generals. "I have already made myself clear. We will continue the air strikes. It is painless, effective and can be maintained indefinitely. ISIL and ISIS have too many soldiers on the ground. Al Kaeta is recruiting again from Asia. We will not know or recognise the enemy on the ground anymore. There are too many of them. Our aim is to support the Government of Iraq fight the terrorists by knocking out their best. Their leaders, their tanks, their machines guns and so on".

The President paused for effect.

"As we speak, there is a secret mission, on its way to try and knock out the top from the terrorist organisation. That is where the money and equipment is coming from. You should be aware that you may be called upon in the last minute to lend a hand. So put all your personnel in the Middle East and Europe on alert. They may be called upon to send a plane, helicopter, special forces, equipment and so on. That is all you need to know at this stage".

The President stood up. All the Generals and others in the room stood up and clicked their heels at attention and saluted smartly. The President returned the salute.

"Gentlemen". He said as he moved towards the door.

The meeting was a brief one. The President bid them farewell and made his way outside to his waiting helicopter. The meeting will continue without him on their strategies in the middle east.

When the hunt for Osama Bin Laden was over, after 10 years, the President was advised that there may be a "double". So the hunt will continue for Osama's double....quietly. The media will be kept guessing...they will not be given any information. Even if the hunt is successful.

Some people say he...the double.... is the real culprit. Osama Bin Laden was just a front. The guy in the shadows is the real man.

It was becoming clear to the Americans that the important men in the terrorist organisations are never seen or heard in public. They are always in the shadows. They have no ids, no bank accounts, no properties....nothing. But they have immense wealth and power in the names of their doubles. They use their properties, bank cards, vehicles, planes...everything.

When trouble arises the doubles are the ones who get arrested while the real masterminds remain in the shadows. They simply create a new double and discard the old one. If the double becomes troublesome they shoot them in the head and create another one. So it is very, very difficult for the men and women in the Secret Services to work out who is responsible for what. Even if Al Kaeta claims responsibility for bombings in Tel Aviv....you can be sure it is not them who did it. It may have been a nice tourist who flew in from London with some marbles that cannot be detected by current technology. He or she just leaves a nice looking marble in a closed empty paper cup in a posh restaurant and push the button on it. It explodes a few minutes later as he or she gets out of there. Al Kaeta simply claims their suicide bomber did it, which cannot be proven...or will be difficult to refute under the circumstances.

"Gentlemen"....the Chief of Staff began..."there is a new proposal for us to consider. This is in regards to the use of surveillance and air strikes using UFOs. The "unidentified flying objects" is a new design by one of our contractors. Each UFO will be able to patrol the target area for up to a month.... 24/7, before it needs refueling. The UFO will be armed with laser technology which has the same devastating effect of a missile. The laser fuel can last for the life of the UFO which is estimated to be 5 years. New ones will be introduced. This is our new approach to conflicts around the world where we are required to help or keep the peace. They are also under remote control. They can be manoeuvred into new positions or to shoot down enemy aircraft or bases on the ground. The laser can pierce heavy armor like tanks and ships so it will be our best helper in the war against terror".

The Chief of Staff looked around at the Generals who were reading the report of the UFO tests.

"Do we agree to give this important and irreplaceable piece of hardware the go ahead?". They were unanimous. The US Army really need something to turn the advantage their way without sending thousands of American soldiers to be maimed and killed in the name of some other country's....often.... commercial interest.

"Sir"...General David Petraeus, former commander in Afganistan, began..."I believe this is the new wave of American technological warfare. We can send out a

thousand UFOs to exterminate up to a
million of the enemy's forces without
putting a single American soldier at risk. I
support it wholeheartedly and I am sure we
have all agreed on it. I however, request,
that its deployment is brought forward from
5 years to as soon as possible. Things may
be different in 5 years. The enemy may have
won the war before we even deploy them. I
ask that we send them out to the field to-day.
Thank you".

The Chief of Staff looked around the large
round table. Everyone was nodding.
"Alright. We have approved its deployment
to-day".

Outside the Pentagon, a rabbit was running
around in circles...feeding on bits of grass
and plants then run under the bushes,
crossed the road and disappeared into a
waiting car. The car sped off and joined the
busy mid-day traffic.

A blonde Caucasian man with an expensive
black suit, heavy duty gloves and a large

diamond studded watch and rings was
stroking the rabbits back. "Good boy"....as
he took off a small metal bead attached to
the rabbit's long fur. He inserted it into his
mobile phone, pressed a number and
listened on the earphones. After a few
minutes he smiled....laughed...then put the
phone in his glove box. He pressed a button
and spoke into the microphone. "Take me to
the airport". The driver turned the car in the
direction of their private runway and
increased the speed.

Professor Doug Shortpines was sitting in his
lab at Georgetown University, Washington.
He was told the UFO project will go ahead.
He was delighted. It has been his dream
since he read the "War of the World" in his
High School days. He thought that wars can
be carried out by machines instead of human
soldiers. He had protested against the war in
Afganistan when too many of their soldiers
were brought back covered in a flag. That
was five years ago. Now his pet project will
take off. He stood up grabbed his hat and
jacket and walked down to his car. They

will meet the manufacturers to ensure specifications are correct. An order for 5,000 UFOs has come through from the Pentagon. The prototype has been tested and approved.

Professor Shortpines was the Chairman of the Board of Directors of TechUSA, the fastest growing war technology company in the world.

The Professor started his SUV and backed out of the carpark. He got on to Reservoir Road and headed towards West Potomac Park. He is to meet a certain French Professor who will order another 5,000 UFOs for the European Union. They fear the war will spread to Europe so they will be patrolling their borders and shoot anything that looks suspicious. At $US5 million each, the UFOs is making a heap of cash for them already. The orders have gone past $US50 billion already and climbing. Each UFO can be replaced easily or upgraded. Their design is flawless.

The Professor went past the JF Kennedy

Center and was heading towards the Vietnam Veterans Memorial when he heard a noise like air escaping a balloon. That was the last sound he heard.

The explosion brought everyone running. The Police, Ambulance and another black car that slowed down to look at the carnage then sped through towards the Tidal Basin. Everyone were too busy looking at the demolished car to notice the black car slowing and the occupants in Arab clothes looking at them. There was no body to examine. Just the chassis and wheels sitting on the road. It has been blown to bits.

TechUSA announced the death of their Chairman of the Board in a road accident in Washington...on the news that evening. There was a brief exchange of condolences by the University, Politicians and everyone and it was forgotten and swept under the carpet.

The new Chairman of the Board of TechUSA was a Scientist from California.

He was also a Professor and high tech warfare fan. Paul Newman. An accomplished scientist in the field of atomic energy and lasers. Apparently, it was him who came up with the idea of nuclear fueled UFOs with lasers to shoot down anything or something on the ground. It looks like a drone but smaller with a "fat body" hence the UFO label.

The new Chairman was summoned to the Pentagon immediately after Professor Shortpines funeral. They want to know when the UFOs can be delivered and how soon can they be deployed in Afganistan, Iraq, Syria, Palestine and in some parts of Africa like Ethiopia and Somalia where rebels are causing a lot of trouble.

"Mr Chairman...I can assure you that your orders are being manufactured as we speak. TechUSA can deliver 1,000 UFOs every month...so your order will be completed in 5 months. We also have another order from Europe for the same number and we might have to share the orders with them. It will take 12 months to complete all the current orders".....Professor Newman looked around the round table. All the Generals were nodding. They all agree.

The helicopter landed in a small airport in Kiev. There was a refueling truck waiting. Two black cars were also parked a little distance from the truck. Commander George Williams walked over to them and two men in Army Uniform came out. They shook hands and discussed some things quietly often nodding their heads.

James could see they were from the Ukranian army. They are the ones fighting the Russian separatists in Ukraine. When the helicopter was full, Commander Williams shook hands with his counter-parts and returned to the helicopter. The Army Officers remained on the ground and waved to them as the helicopter disappeared into the night sky. They crossed the border into Russia a few hours later.

"Mr Chairman your request for 3 UFOs has been delivered as requested. They will be flown to Kiev and the command post will be setup there. I have no more involvement as your Officers will take over". Professor Newman stood up and bowed slightly then walked out the door.

The meeting continued without him.

"Mr Chairman, all the arrangements have been made. Our mission will arrive in Moscow tomorrow. They will be briefed tonight at Podol, a small town outside Moscow before their final approach. The Russians know they are some Ukranian businessmen on a business trip to Moscow". The Chief of Intelligence took off his reading glasses and looked around the table. All the Generals were nodding. It has been a long accepted etiquette of army meetings to be very frugal with words.

"Thank you, James. Let's now look at the matter of assessing the new threat in light of our current UFO deployment. It is my belief that the threat will be minimized if not totally eliminated. Our concern of course, is not to turn this into "Moslems vs Christians" or "Palestinians vs Jews" kind of war. I would like to believe that this is a conflict of good against evil. We should be erring on the side of good all the time. The moment we are perceived as an evil nation...the war would be lost even before it begins".

The Chairman looks around the table. All the Generals were nodding their heads.

"Well, it seems that we all agree, let's have a break for lunch and continue this afternoon".

The Chief of Staff stood up. All the Generals and others in the room stood together and clicked their heels. They salute smartly and head towards the door. The Chief of Staff returned the salute as he went into another room....for a private meeting.

Chapter 8. Number 10 Downing Street.

"Thanks for coming at such short notice"....the Prime Minister David Cameron was standing on the steps outside his Number 10 Downing Street office. "As you all requested .....and I called this quick meeting.....is to update everyone on the war against terror. We, of course, have joined the air strikes and withdrawn troops from the ground. Only advisors and training personnel are still left. The Allies have been joined by France and other European nations in the air strikes against ISIS and ISIL. Our goal is to support the Iraq Government in its fight against the rebels and terrorists. The situation in Syria is not as clear as there are rebels fighting the Syrian Government and we had supported the rebels with the Americans....I will inform you as soon as our information is received on what is happening there". The Prime Minister looks at the small group of journalists listening and taking notes. Several TV cameras were there too.

"Sir, what is the official position of the Government on Afghanistan? Is the war over in Kabul or are there anything left to do over there?"...A journalist from one of the TV news asked.

"Afghanistan has been moved further down our priorities. There are some advisors there, but the local Government is handling most of the local action".

The PM looks around at them and wondered whether there might be any spies among them.

"When is the war on terror going to end Mr Prime Minister? It seems there are new groups rising up of the desert sand and taking the place of the defeated ones. What is the situation in Yemen? Is it true the rebels have overrun the Government over there?"....Another TV News journalist asked and motioned his cameraman to come closer and get the PM's response for the evening news.

"Yes, the situation in Yemen is being resolved politically as we speak. It is true there is a new Government. All parties are in agreement on the way forward for the country so we are not too concerned over them at the moment. One last question please"...the PM looked around and pointed at the back. A young journalist in a tracksuit was taking notes furiously and looking around him frequently. "Sir, is it true the Americans and the Allies are planning to bomb Moscow?"....everyone turned around and looked at him silently in shock.....how could he know that the Allies are planning to bomb Moscow?

"I am sorry what is your name and which paper are you from?". The PM asked him. He looked around quickly and said..."A local paper"...
The PM nodded at the security. "No I have not heard any information about bombings of Moscow. Thank you, everyone."

As the journalists dispersed the security

people moved in and grabbed the young journalist who asked the question about Moscow and led him into an unmarked car. He tried to struggle but he was held with iron clasps. No one seem to notice. The PM was watching and then turned and moved into the building as the guard opens the door.

David Cameron was alarmed. Only a few people know about the Moscow mission...less than 10 in the whole world. They are all top security people and the President and him....yet this young journalist seem to know something about it.

He told the security people to bring the young man and interrogate him while they listen to what he has to say. He got the second shock of his day. The security staff told him the young man collapsed and died....apparently of cyanide poisoning before they asked him a single question!. They think that he might have something in his mouth. He also had an automatic revolver on him.

"He may have planned to use it if you had

said anything about bombings in Russia".

The Head of Security said as he went out the door.

David Cameron just shook his head as he went into his office and closed the door.

The helicopter circled and landed in a small clearing outside a large mansion. It looks like one of the famous mansions in England. Must be a former Nobleman under the Czar, James thought as they disembarked.

A guard was waving at them to come in. A side door was open. It was morning but the sun has not risen yet. The sky was gray and cold. James thought he could see somebody darting around among the trees beside the large mansion lawn and garden and he angled his head towards the trees.

Commander Williams saw it too and nodded. He hurried inside and waved everyone in quickly.
They were shown to a large meeting room in

the basement. Commander Williams insisted on meeting in a room on the first floor. James nodded to the Colonel and disappeared into another room. He took out his binoculars and surveyed the surrounding trees and fields. They were surrounded by Russian soldiers! He came back and sat down beside Commander Williams at the table and shoved a note under his notepad. Commander Williams moved his book aside and read it. "Surrounded by Russian Army!".

He looked at James and shook his head then put his hand to his ear. James understood. He moved back and sneaked out of the room into the toilet. He brought out his satellite phone and rang the emergency number. He gave them the details, then went back into the room.

"Let's begin our meeting shall we?". One of the leaders in the new group that came in said and stood up. He wore a warm tracksuit, as if he has been running. James has no doubt that the group which joined them are Russian spies.

"Commander Williams my name is General Bob Spiers of the US Army we will provide the backup. You and your group will be flown, by helicopter, and deposited a few metres from the Kremlin at Red Square. It will be tonight so there will be a few people around.   We will cordon the whole area off so no one gets in the way. You are to move straight into the Kremlin and take over the building. You will be given instructions tomorrow, once the Kremlin is secured. We will provide the security.

James looked at Commander Williams, he nodded.

This Russian guy is pretty good. He has an American accent as well.

"We have provided some light snacks at the back of the room and you will be shown to your rooms for resting then we move tonight". General Spiers continued as he surveyed their group, probably making a mental note of what they look like, in case they meet later by accident.

"Please enjoy your meal and I will meet you outside, when the helicopters arrive".

James was really uneasy. He joined Angie as they nibbled on the snacks. They all nod at each other. It was a trap!

James and Angie moved into one room as they were shown their quarters. The satellite phone beeped. James picked it up as they lay on the bed. The message say...."in case you are arrested and locked in a room we will transfer the control of the UFOs to you. They are the latest "drone tech" available to the US Army. They can remain airborne for a month and has the latest laser which can pierce tank armor"....the satellite phone beeped then went out.

James has no idea what they are, but he is familiar with drones...so he got on to the idea quickly. He put away his satellite phone.

"Now, my dear, is our finest hour....let's

make love and be merry for tomorrow may be our last"....James smiled as Angie met his kiss. It was always heaven to kiss that girl. She is so warm and tender...her body so inviting. He just got lost in the passion and forgot about the danger.

Later as they lie in bed, spent from their passion. Angie asked the expected question. "Why do you think they have not arrested us?". James looked at her thoughtfully. "Beats me. I think Mr Vladimir Putin is just having some fun".

David Cameron picked up the ringing phone. "I'm afraid our mission has been compromised. Our operatives are in a Mansion in Podol, outside Moscow, surrounded by the Russian Army but they are pretending not to notice. They will be dropped off at Red Square tonight where I suppose the Russians will have fun shooting them down. That is my assessment of the situation"....David Cameron looked really sick as he put the phone down. He barely mumbled.

"Yes, I understand, Mr President".

David Cameron picked up another secure phone and dialed a number.

"Can you please connect me to the Director of MI5?"..."Yes, Sir"...came the answer. The phone rings and somebody answers. "MI5".

"Director. This is the Prime Minister. Can you come around with a plan to rescue our operation in Moscow?".

"Sure Sir". Eric Abbot was always a guy who enjoys a challenge. He picked up the pre-planned rescue plan and called his driver.

"10 Downing Street please".

The driver took off with screeching tyres. He knows Eric like a bit a drama.

"Thank you driver that was an excellent take off". Eric smiled.

"Thank you, Sir". The driver beamed.

Chapter 9. The Kremlin

The Kremlin had been under fire in the stand off with President Boris Yeltsin before. President Yeltsin had ordered the tanks to fire on the Kremlin to force parliament to surrender. The whole team have read about it. But they are wondering now, what to do. If the President can order the tanks to fire on the Kremlin, surely a few Allied spies trying to steal information will be shot on sight.

They did not like the idea at all. They have checked their sub-machine guns. They are ready for a shoot out with the Russians in Red Square which will end in their demise as there are only 14 of them and 143 million Russians waiting.

James kissed Angie on the cheek and she turned her head up and faced him. He kissed her again on the lips...slowly. She closed her eyes. They always sit at the back so they can do anything without the others watching. They looked down from the helicopter to the lights of Moscow as they approach and circle lower onto Red Square. Now is the hour. James thought....when we say goodbye. He kissed Angie again and said in her ear...."Keep close to me. When the shooting starts".

The helicopter landed in the Middle of Red Square. They got out quickly and ran crouching their sub-machine guns towards the Kremlin. Nothing happened. They were getting more and more suspicious as they got closer to the building.

A guard was standing near an open door and motioned them to go in. They went through a long corridor then through several doors into a hall. It was about 20 metres by 40 metres and decorated with Christian motifs. Gold and silver paint was used on the door decorations and large paintings of Lenin and Putin were hung on the wall. There was no one there. They stood around looking, not knowing what to do. Then a side door opened and Osama Bin Laden walked out! They were all shocked! He was dressed just like the TV pictures.

"He looks more like Rasputin from the stories of the Czarina and Czar Nicholas"...James whispered to Angie.

"Good evening Gentlemen. You have come to find me or information about my operations. You shall have it". He said it in the same tone as he used to say things on TV.

Commander Williams recovered from his shock and addressed Mr Bin Laden.

"We are not sure who you are or what you are doing here, Sir. Maybe you can explain for the benefit of all". Commander Williams looked around a bit embarrassed then looked back at Mr Bin Laden.

"Well, obviously, I am the real Bin Laden. The man you killed was my double. I am responsible for the war in the Middle East as you no doubt gathered so far. I provide equipment and funds to all supporters of Islam and to good causes, by deserving

Moslems".

They all stood with their sub-machine guns facing this lone Arab dressed like a Prince of Arabia and not knowing what to do. The man admits all the war crimes they are looking for, yet they feel some kind of admiration for him. They have hunted him for more than 10 years then killed the wrong guy. Now here he is in front of them unarmed admitting it all. And they have sub-machine guns but no will to use it!.

Commander Williams spoke. "If you are the man responsible for all the war atrocities in the Middle East, what are you doing in the Kremlin?".

"I simply hired the Russian soldiers and the hall for this purpose Commander Williams. The Russians understand my predicament and are sympathetic to the desperation of our people, so they feel it is wiser for us to talk about it face to face here. I am sure you are shocked. So go back to your masters in the West and tell them what I told you".

Osama Bin Laden bowed and disappeared through the door where he came through. Then they heard a helicopter taking off. They were frozen, not knowing what to do. All the information and proof has been handed to them.

"If you guys are finished, let's go back to Podol now where you will be flown back to Kiev.   A commercial flight will take you to Istanbul where you will receive your instructions".

The man who spoke to them obviously knew about their previous instructions. He has gone out the door too.

"Alright. Let's do what he says. I have nothing further to add. We are going to hand in our weapons to the British Embassy at Istanbul and disperse". Commander Williams was looking totally bewildered. This was a turn of events unexpected by anyone. This guy....who claim to be Osama Bin Laden.... obviously operates like a divine being. He seem to be above everything and everyone, yet is a humble man when he speaks. George thought, it must be time to retire. Either he is dreaming or watching a spy movie.

They all trooped outside, looking a bit deflated and got into the helicopter which took off back to Podol.

"What do you think?". James whispered to Angie. "I am glad. I think we should retire darling. We are just soldiers. Let the Politicians handle the war. Let's settle down and have kids. I would love to have as many kids I can handle". She giggled and snuggled up to him as the helicopter gained speed and altitude. He put his hand around her and closed his eyes.

A flash of lightning seared his eyeballs as if by a nuclear blast. He opened his eyes and looked back just in time to see another laser beam hit the Kremlin and it burst into flames then like flashlights going on and off from the sky.

"Beams of lightning", as the locals call it, started fires all over Moscow. James took out his satellite phone and turned it on. He put it on TV and watched Moscow from space, zooming in on the Kremlin. The building is on fire and fire engines are heading towards it. Beams of light are zooming down from space ....buildings explodes and burst into flame as they got hit. Everyone else seem to be unaware of what is going on. He is the only one in the back seat and he noticed it. He understood what is going on.

Then beams of missiles and guns firing starts on the ground heading up to space. James can count more than a 100 UFOs blowing up buildings all over Moscow and the Russians returning the fire, but probably unaware of what they are. They probably thought they are planes but cannot hear anything.

Their helicopter continued on to Podol completely. Unaware of what is going on in

Moscow.

"I think you are right honey. Let's settle down and have some kids. I do love kids myself. Leave the war to the Politicians".

James kissed Angie and for a moment thought that Ada was looking up at him.

They all went straight to bed on arrival in Podol. The appetite for war completely, knocked out of them, while the UFOs lay waste to a few buildings in Moscow before disappearing into the night.

They were on the helicopter again the next morning heading for Podol Airport. They will fly from there instead of Kiev.   James and Angie have given up guessing as to what will happen next. It's as if somebody is pulling all the strings in their game and they are doing all the dancing.

The plane was a small Russian made jet aircraft. It was very comfortable inside. There were about 20 seats in total. They were handed refreshments and breakfast by a very pretty Russian stewardess. She kept looking at James and Angie and smiling. She can tell straight away that they are in love. Every girl dreams of falling in love with a guy like James....even a tough, pretty girl like Angie.

They slept all the way to Istanbul!

They were put in a hotel in downtown Istanbul while the situation was being assessed.

They watched the English news on TV from London the next morning.

The report showed large number of buildings that were destroyed in Moscow or were still burning during the night. It suggests there were different factions of the Russian military who were fighting each other over control of the Kremlin. They also said that it is possible terrorists had attacked the Kremlin and went off with large amounts of highly classified documents.

President Vladimir Putin did not make any comments. Instead, the Kremlin gave the media a statement that it is investigating all the claims.

The media went on to say...."it seems that whoever attacked Moscow, whether they were factions of the Russian military or terrorists have vanished into thin air!"...

The news media also suggested there was also a rumor that Allied Commandos landed in Red Square and carried out the attacks on the Kremlin.

They all looked at each other and fell over laughing. Lucky they got out in time!

Chapter 10. A little place near the Sea.

James and Angie boarded the Queen Elizabeth II in Auckland, New Zealand. It was cruising around the Pacific Islands. Auckland, Tonga, Samoa, Fiji, Vanuatu, New Caledonia, Solomon Is, Sydney and Brisbane in Australia, Papua New Guinea, Palau, Micronesia, Marshalls, Hawaii, San Francisco and San Diego in USA and back to the Pacific.

They had flown from Paris to London to be debriefed then Washington to pick up their "rewards". On the way to the airport they opened them they were 2 motels in Auckland, New Zealand. A nice city in the Pacific, far away from the war...where they can have as many kids as they want.

James and Angie were given a room on the top of the QEII where they can view all the going ons down below...swimming pool, bar, dancing floor. They were watching the dancing down below when the announcer

called everyone's attention..."Ladies and
Gentlemen I am pleased to be the bearer of
good tidings. James Bonaparte is asking
Angelique Royal to marry him tonight.
Everyone clapped and moved on to the floor.
Angie was caught by surprise! She turned
around and James was on one knee with a
ring in his hand. "Will you marry me my
angel?"...he said with a slight smile but
serious face. Everyone was quite. They all
want to hear her answer. "Yes!" she shouted.
"Yes, my darling". She kissed him as he
stood up and put the ring on her finger while
everyone clapped from the dance floor
below.

Then the band played James's favourite
waltz by Elvis Presley..."Are you lonesome
tonight?"....while they dance on the top deck
and everyone else danced on the floor below.

James and Angie announced their wedding
on the ship in Noumea in New Caledonia.
They will have a French wedding on shore
with all the QEII guests invited.
James stopped the car in front of two large

mango trees. They got off and he pointed up to a little bungalow with a large veranda about 10 metres from the road.

"That my darling is my little place facing the sea". He turned around and pointed to the sea down below. It was the best view she has seen in a long time.

"I just built the veranda a few months ago when our plan to come here was confirmed. We can enjoy the view from there with our meals. There are two rooms, kitchen, bathroom and toilet. I think its good enough for awhile until the babies arrive!"

Angie looked at the little house and the sea below and she had tears in her eyes. I love it, my darling. We can stay here during the holidays and spent the hot summer in one of our motels in Auckland".

"Whatever you say darling, this is our little corner of the world". James walked up to the door and put in the key, twisted the knob and disappeared inside. Angie followed.

They went into the bedroom and turned on the air condition.

"It is perfect dear. I love it already".She has a wide grin on her face. She gave him a hug and kiss then moved to the window.

"Let's go and get some shopping and fill the shopping cupboard". James picked up a large bamboo basket for the shopping. "Remind me to pick some mangoes for breakfast". James said as he pointed at the huge bunches of mangoes on the large trees.

"Hmmm...I can eat as many as 5 in one go". She laughed, thinking of her days in Africa when mangoes was a large part of her diet.

The next day they tuned in to the news on the radio while having breakfast in bed. The BBC which has an international service around the Pacific has announced that Russia has retaliated to the attack on the Kremlin by firing two nuclear warheads towards the United States. The rockets will take some time to reach their destinations, but it is a very clear declaration of war. The British are not sure whether they will be fired on, although no statements have come out of the Kremlin.

They looked at each other in shocked silence.

"Oh my God!". She put her right hand to her eyes as tears welled up.

"Its a good thing we came here honey, to be far away from the war ....as far away as possible". James whispered to Angie as they lay on the bed listening to the terrible news.

Then another international report at noon suggest that there is no contact with Russia whatsoever and there are more then 100 nuclear warheads already fired from Russia heading in different directions as picked up by the NATO surveillance units around Europe.

The Americans and NATO have fired interceptor missiles to explode the rockets in the air. No one knows yet what will happen if all the nuclear warheads explode in the air.

They are also testing a "capture" missile which will capture the incoming missiles with the nuclear warheads and bring them down via parachute. Military teams from the Allies will pick them up and dismantled by their experts.

All commercial flights around the world have ceased.

"Thank you, darling. Thank you for bringing me here. I feel safe and at home, whatever the future may bring as a result of this war. Angie looked at James, with tears in her eyes, and he could see that she really means it.

THE END...

Some notes for the reader...on the various organisations...and governments mentioned .

Summarized from Wikipedia, the free online encyclopedia.

ISIL and ISIS

The Islamic State of Iraq and Syria (ISIS), is a Sunni, extremist, jihadist rebel group controlling territory in Iraq, Syria, eastern Libya and the Sinai Peninsula of Egypt.

The group's actions have been widely criticized around the world with many Islamic communities describing the group as not representing Islam. The United Nations and Amnesty International have accused ISIL of grave human rights abuses, and Amnesty International has found it guilty of ethnic cleansing on a "historic scale". ISIL has been designated as a terrorist organization by the United Nations, the European Union, the United Kingdom, the United States, Australia, Canada, Turkey,

Saudi Arabia, Indonesia, the UAE and Israel.

The group originated in 1999, which became commonly known as Al-Baeda in Iraq in 2004. Following the 2003 invasion of Iraq, AQI took part in the Iraqi insurgency. In 2006, it joined other Sunni insurgent groups to form the Mujahideen Shura Council, which consolidated further into the Islamic State of Iraq (ISI) shortly afterwards. ISI gained a significant presence in Al Anbar, Nineveh, Kirkuk and other areas, but around 2008, its violent methods, including suicide attacks on civilian targets and the widespread killing of prisoners, led to a backlash from Sunni Iraqis and other insurgent groups.

In April 2013, the group changed its name to the Islamic State of Iraq and the Levant (ISIL). It grew significantly after entering the Syrian Civil War, it established a large presence in the Syrian governorates of Ar-Raqqah,Idlib, Deir ez-Zor and Aleppo. ISIL had close links to al-Qaeda until February 2014.

The PLO

The Palestine Liberation Organization was founded in 1964 with the purpose of the "liberation of Palestine" through armed struggle. It is recognized as the "sole" legitimate representative of Palestinians by over 100 states with which it holds diplomatic relations and has enjoyed observer status at the United Nations since 1974.The PLO was considered by the United States and Israel to be a terrorist organization until 1991. In 1993, the PLO recognized Israel's right to exist and accepted the UN Security Council resolutions 242 and 338 which rejects violence and terrorism.

The Palestinian territories include the Westbank and the Gaza Strip. An area of 6,000 square km with about 4 million people.

Israel

The League of Nations had given the British the mandate over Palestine in 1920, had no desire to confront local Arab gangs that frequently attacked Palestinian Jews. Believing that they could not rely on the British administration for protection from these gangs, the Jewish leadership created the Haganah to protect Jewish farms and in addition to guarding Jewish communities, the role of the Haganah was to warn the residents of and repel attacks by Palestinian Arabs.Following the **1929 Palestine riots**, the Haganah's role changed dramatically. It became a much larger organization encompassing nearly all the youth and adults in the Jewish settlements, as well as thousands of members from the cities. It also acquired foreign arms and began to develop workshops to create **hand grenades** and simple military equipment, transforming from an untrained militia to a capable underground army.

On 29 November 1947, the United Nations General Assembly recommended the adoption and implementation of the Partition Plan for Mandatory Palestine. The end of the British Mandate for Palestine was set for midnight on 14 May 1948. That day, David Ben-Gurion, the Executive Head of the Zionist Organization and president of the Jewish Agency for Palestine, declared "the establishment of a Jewish state in Eretz Israel, to be known as the State of Israel," which would start to function from the termination of the mandate. The borders of the new state were not specified. Neighboring Arab armies invaded the former Palestinian mandate on the next day and fought the Israeli forces. Israel has since fought several wars with neighboring Arab states,in the course of which it has occupied the West Bank, Sinai Peninsula (1956–1957, 1967–1982), part of South Lebanon (1982–2000), Gaza Strip and the Golan Heights. It extended its laws to the Golan Heights and East Jerusalem, but not the West Bank. Israel has signed peace treaties with Egypt and with Jordan, but efforts to resolve the

Israeli–Palestinian conflict have so far not resulted in peace.

The IRA

The IRA (Irish Republican Army) is a name used to describe several armed movements in Ireland in the 20th and 21st centuries. All claim descent from the original Irish Republican Army, which was formed from the Irish Volunteers. It was the army of the Irish Republic in 1919. Most Irish people dispute the claims of more recently created organizations.

For the IRA, that has constantly been the case. The first split came after the Anglo-Irish Treaty in 1921, with supporters of the Treaty forming the nucleus of the National Army of the newly created Free State, while the anti-treaty forces continued to use the name *Irish Republican Army*. After the end of the Irish Civil War, the IRA was around in one form or another for forty years, when it split into the Official IRA and the Provisional IRA   in 1969. The latter then had its own breakaways, namely the Real IRA and the Continuity IRA, each claiming to be the true successor of the Army of the Irish Republic.

The Muslim Brotherhood

The Society of the Muslim Brothers shortened to the Muslim Brotherhood is a transnational Islamist organization which was founded in Egypt in 1928 by the Islamic scholar and schoolteacherHassan al-Banna.The motto of the Brotherhood was traditionally "Believers are but Brothers". That was expanded into a five-part slogan: "God is our objective; the Quran is the Constitution; the Prophet is our leader; jihad is our way; death for the sake of God is our wish." It began as a Pan-Islamic, religious, and social movement. The Muslim Brotherhood had an estimated two million members by the end of World War II. Evidence of its vast influence was clear, with more than 2,000 branches all over the country and 2,000 societies for charity and social services. It ran health clinics, sports clubs, schools and other educational institutes, mosques and Islamic centres, and had a presence of 10,000 army volunteers in Palestine.Its ideas had gained supporters throughout the Arab world and influenced other Islamist groups with its "model of political activism combined with Islamic charity work". In 2012, it became the first democratically elected political party in Egypt, but it is considered a terrorist organization by the governments of Bahrain, Egypt, Russia, Syria, Saudi Arabia and United Arab Emirates. However, the Brotherhood insists it is a peaceful organisation, pointing to its democratic elections, and has consistently renounced violence.Its top leader is on record as saying that the group "condemns violence and violent acts".

The Brotherhood's stated goal is to instill the Qur'an and Sunnah as the "sole reference point for ... ordering the life of the Muslim family, individual, community ... and state.The Muslim Brotherhood is financed by contributions from its members, who are required to allocate a portion of their income to the movement. Some of these contributions are from members who work in Saudi Arabia and other oil-rich countries.

The Pentagon

The Pentagon is the headquarters of the United States Department of Defense, located in Arlington County, Virginia. As a symbol of the U.S. military, "the Pentagon" is often used metonymically to refer to the U.S. Department of Defense.

The Pentagon is a large office building, with approximately 23,000 military and civilian employees and about 3,000 non-defense support personnel work in the Pentagon. It has five sides, five floors above ground, two basement levels, and five ring corridors per floor with a total of 17.5 miles of corridors. The Pentagon includes a five-acre central plaza, which is shaped like a pentagon and informally known as "ground zero," a nickname originating during the Cold War on the presumption that it would be targeted by the Soviet Union at the outbreak of nuclear war.

On September 11, 2001, exactly 60 years after the building's construction began, American Airlines Flight 77 was hijacked and flown into the Western side of the building, killing 189 people including the five hijackers.It was the first significant foreign attack on the capital's governmental facilities since the burning of Washington during the War of 1812.

Number 10 Downing Street

10 Downing Street, colloquially known in the United Kingdom as "Number 10", is the headquarters of the British Government and the official residence and office of the First Lord of the Treasury, an office now invariably held by the Prime Minister.

Situated in Downing Street in the City of Westminster, London, Number 10 is one of the most famous addresses in the world. Over three hundred years old, the building contains about one hundred rooms. There is a private residence on the third floor and a kitchen in the basement. The other floors contain offices and numerous conference, reception, sitting and dining rooms where the Prime Minister works, and where government ministers, national leaders and foreign dignitaries are met and entertained. There is an interior courtyard and, in the back, a terrace overlooking a garden of 0.5 acres. Adjacent to St. James's Park, Number 10 is near to Buckingham Palace, the official London residence of the British monarch, and the Palace of Westminster, the meeting place of both houses of parliament.

The Kremlin

The Moscow Kremlin, is usually referred to as simply the Kremlin, is a historic fortified complex at the heart of Moscow, overlooking the Moskva River to the south, Saint Basil's Cathedral and Red Square to the east, and the Alexander Garden to the west. It is the best known of kremlins (Russian citadels) and includes five palaces, four cathedrals, and the enclosing Kremlin Wall with Kremlin towers. The complex serves as the official residence of the President of the Russian Federation.

The name *Kremlin* means "fortress inside a city", and is often used as a metonym to refer to the government of the Russian Federation in a similar sense to how the *White House* is used to refer to the Executive Office of the President of the United States. It had previously been used to refer to the government of the Soviet Union (1922–1991) and its highest members (such as general secretaries, premiers, presidents, ministers, and commissars).

NATO

The North Atlantic Treaty Organization (NATO), also called the North Atlantic Alliance; is an intergovernmental military alliance based on the North Atlantic Treaty which was signed on 4 April 1949. The organization constitutes a system of collective defence whereby its member states agree to mutual defense in response to an attack by any external party. NATO's headquarters are in Brussels, Belgium, one of the 28 member states across North America and Europe, the newest of which, Albania and Croatia, joined in April 2009. An additional 22 countries participate in NATO's "Partnership for Peace" program, with 15 other countries involved in institutionalized dialogue programmes. The combined military spending of all NATO members constitutes over 70 percent of the global total.Members' defense spending is supposed to amount to 2 percent of GDP.

A STATEMENT FROM THE AUTHOR...

World peace is a concern for all the citizens of the world. I hope this story will contribute in some small way towards world peace.

We, the citizens of the earth, have a responsibility to the future generations to preserve and enhance their inheritance. Whether they be the environment, education, health, the world economy or world peace.

The earth cannot survive a nuclear war. In fact, it will not survive continued armed disagreements between religions and races or global warming.

We all have to work together to solve the age old differences among the races and religions of the Middle East.

May the future generations inherit nothing but peace and prosperity from the current caretakers of the earth.

Notes on the author...

 Semisi Pone graduated from the University of Auckland in 1985 with a BSc and in 1989 with a MSc (Hons). He has worked as a Scientist in the Pacific for about 10 years and has travelled extensively during that time. He did some work for MAFF, Tonga. University of the South Pacific, Samoa. South Pacific Commission, Fiji. He was also appointed to one of the Food and Agriculture Organisation of the United Nations expert panels for 3 years in 1993 and a further 4 years in 1996.

He has written more than 70 books and ebooks. They can be found by searching his name in the websites of amazon.com, blurb.com, apple.com and wheelers.co.nz. There are others who also sell his books in New Zealand and globally.